CRANBERRY ♥ VALENTINE

Wende and Harry Berlin

FOUR WINDS PRESS
New York

FOUR WINDS PRESS
Macmillan Publishing Company
866 Third Avenue, New York, N.Y. 10022
Collier Macmillan Canada, Inc.

Printed and bound by South China Printing Company, Hong Kong
First American Edition

10 9 8 7 6 5 4 3 2

The text of this book is set in 14 pt. Baskerville.
The illustrations are rendered in watercolor.

Library of Congress Cataloging-in-Publication Data

Devlin, Wende.
Cranberry Valentine.

Summary: Maggie, her grandmother, and the sewing
circle make Cranberryport a brighter place for
Mr. Whiskers when they send him secret valentines.
[1. Valentines—Fiction.   2. Valentine's Day—
Fiction.   3. Friendship—Fiction]   I. Devlin, Harry.
II. Title.
PZ7.D49875Cu 1986   [E]   85-24047
ISBN 0-02-729200-2

For Julia Wende Gates

It was a gray February day in Cranberryport, and the warm fire was welcome in Grandmother's kitchen.

Maggie, Grandmother and Mr. Whiskers sat around the table amid ribbon, lace and pink hearts. Maggie was making valentines for her friends. Valentine's Day was only a week away.

Mr. Whiskers, Maggie's friend and neighbor, looked wistful.

"When I was in school, no one ever sent *me* a valentine," he said. "Never!"

Later, after Mr. Whiskers had returned to his little gray cottage over the dunes, Maggie spoke to Grandmother.

"Poor Mr. Whiskers. I feel sorry for him. He's *never* gotten a valentine," she said.

Grandmother was in a rush. "I'm off to my sewing circle, Maggie. Can we talk about it tonight?"

Two days later, Mr. Whiskers's fortune had changed.
But he didn't think it was for the better!

"It's terrible, Maggie! Look what somebody sent me!"
He stood at Maggie's door in a fury and waved a frothy
lace valentine in the air.

"It's all about cupids, lovebirds, hearts and flowers. And it smells like rose perfume." He wrinkled his nose.

"How sweet," said Maggie.

"Revolting," said Mr. Whiskers. "Who did it?"

"I wonder if it could have been that lady in a green coat. Yesterday, she asked me where you lived," said Maggie.

Mr. Whiskers didn't worry too much until he received three more fragrant valentines at the Cranberryport Post Office the very next day. He quickly hid them under his coat. *Now* Mr. Whiskers was getting nervous.

At Seth's General Store, two more greetings for Mr. Whiskers appeared mysteriously.

"Gosh! Listen to this one, Mr. Whiskers," cried Seth.

"Little cupid shot his dart.
　　Love for you has filled my heart!
　　Be my valentine."

Mr. Whiskers turned red and hid his face behind the mops.

"Say, all week some lady in a green coat has been in here asking questions about you," said Seth.

"Suffering codfish! Somebody's after me," groaned Mr. Whiskers.

"Could be," said Seth.

"Why me?" asked Mr. Whiskers. Then he reflected, "Why not? I'm the best clam digger in the bog country. I have wonderful whiskers. I sing like a blinking bird."

Seth broke into Mr. Whiskers's shining thoughts. "Now, Mr. Whiskers, if some lady gives you a present on this Valentine's Day, you should have a box of chocolates to give in return. A gentleman would."

Mr. Whiskers looked terrified at the idea.

Seth chose a red-satin, heart-shaped box and handed it to his friend. At the sound of the door opening, the storekeeper looked up.

"Oh! Here comes the lady who has been looking for you," said Seth. "Ma'am, I'd like to introduce Mr. Whiskers."

The lady in the green coat! Mr. Whiskers froze! He was trapped. Trapped like a fly in a honey pot.

The lady in the green coat flew across the room to him.

"Aha! Mr. Whiskers at last! I've been looking for you everywhere. I hear you are the best man in town to fix an old chimney."

"Fix a chimney? That's all? I mean—it will be a pleasure, ma'am."

When the lady in green left, Mr. Whiskers did a little sailor's jig. "Saved!" he cried. "I'll give the candy to Maggie and Grandmother," he decided.

He whistled all the way to their house on the edge of the bog.

At the door he bowed deeply to Maggie. "Candy for
my best friends," he announced.

"Come in," said Maggie. "Look, Grandmother, Mr. Whiskers has a present for the whole sewing circle."

Mr. Whiskers heard a hum of voices in the parlor.
"Well, I don't know." Mr. Whiskers hesitated.

"Candy for all of us?" asked Grandmother.

Irving Berlin

The ladies in the circle stopped their sewing and looked up. They began to smile.

"How did you know it was the sewing circle who was sending all those valentines? We've been busy trying to keep you guessing, and all the time you knew it was us!" declared Grandmother.

Mr. Whiskers shuffled his feet.

Suddenly, he put it all together. These were the secret admirers who had scared him with valentines. He drew a breath.

"Knew? Of course, I knew!" he sputtered. "Suffering codfish, you can't fool an old seabird like me!"

Grandmother seated him near the fire with tea and cake.

When the red-satin box was passed, he poked four chocolates before he found one with a caramel filling. Grandmother pretended not to see.

Mr. Whiskers beamed. It wasn't so bad to be the valentine of a whole sewing circle, he decided. Valentine's Day could be a wonderful day for people to think of one another. Now he could hardly wait for next year.

Cranberry Upside-Down Cake
(Get Mother to help)

1 box of yellow cake mix
4 to 5 cups of raw cranberries
2½ cups of white sugar
1 cup of brown sugar
1 stick of butter (¼ lb.)
1 cup of walnut halves or pieces

Preheat oven to 350°.

Slice the stick of butter in thin pieces. Distribute the pieces evenly over the bottom of a 9-by-12-inch pan or a large round one. Sprinkle the walnut halves or pieces over the butter. Wash and dry the cranberries, and pour them over the nuts. Add the white sugar and the brown sugar, spreading evenly over the cranberries. Mix the sugar and the cranberries slightly.

Follow the directions on the box to prepare the yellow cake mixture, and pour it over everything. Bake at 350° for 40 to 50 minutes (It's done when a toothpick inserted in the center comes out clean).

Let cool for 10 minutes. Then, with a knife, loosen the cake from the edges of the pan, and turn the pan over on a plate. Serve with whipped cream or vanilla ice cream.